THE GOOD HAIR DAY

Words by Christian Trimmer

Pictures by J Yang

S0-AZI-583

ABRAMS BOOKS FOR YOUNG READERS | NEW YORK

Noah's birthday was just around the corner.

To make sure he got what he wanted,
he planted subtle hints.

"I really want **THIS**," he told his mom.

"I really, really have to have **THAT**," he said to his dad.

"And **THIS?**" he cried to his sister.
"Come on—I'll die if I don't get it!"
But the thing Noah wanted more than *anything* . . .

WAS LONG HAIR.

Long, beautiful, wavy hair.
Hair that he could braid and twist and
pile on top of his head.

Hair that he could toss back and forth during dance parties with his dad.

Hair that would catch the wind and flow in a magical train behind him.

Hair so thick and long that he could hang from trees with it.

But all Noah's hair would do
is this.

And this.

Each morning, he'd watch as his sister pulled her locks into a tight ponytail.

(It was always off-center, which made Noah cringe.)

And each night, he'd quietly observe his mother as she brushed her hair.

He loved weekends best.
On Saturday mornings, his sister
would let him braid her hair before
she headed off to soccer.
In the safety of his sister's room,
Noah would don his favorite T-shirt.

And on Saturday nights, he would stroke his
mom's hair as the family watched a movie.
But oh, to have long hair
of his very own!

Noah understood that if he just didn't get a haircut, his hair would get longer. But something kept him from asking his parents if he could let his hair grow.

Maybe it was because he once heard some people say mean things about men with long hair.

Or maybe it was because almost every boy
he knew had short hair.
His dad had short hair.
So did his grandpa,
his uncle,
his cousin,
his second cousin,
his teacher,
the mailman,
the guy who bagged the groceries,
and pretty much everyone in his class.
The principal at school had hair so short, he was bald!

And even though his down-the-street neighbor and one of his friends from tennis camp had long hair, he just didn't think he was allowed to ask for it.

So, with a heavy heart, Noah gave his wish list to his mom, and then he left with his dad to get his birthday haircut.

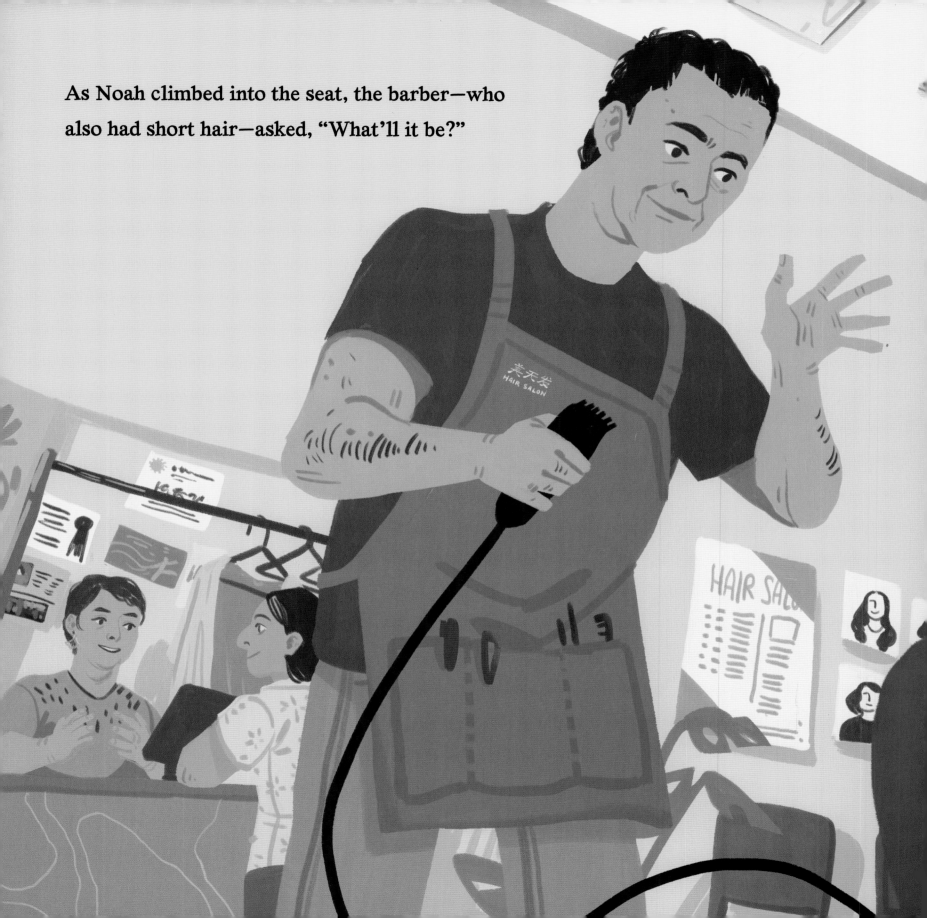

As Noah climbed into the seat, the barber—who also had short hair—asked, "What'll it be?"

Noah wanted to scream, "Don't cut any of my hair!"
But the words wouldn't find their way out of his mouth.
He heard his dad say, "He'll have the usual."

When the barber was done, Noah couldn't help it—
he burst into tears.

That night, after his bath, he wrapped a towel around his head the way he'd seen his mom do. He liked the way it looked.

And the next morning at breakfast,
he wore his favorite T-shirt
downstairs for the first time ever.

On his birthday, Noah woke up excited, because—
let's be real—it was his birthday!

His grandma got him
THIS,

and the neighbors got him
THAT.

But what was
in this box?

He couldn't believe his
sister actually got him
THIS.

Noah ripped off the ribbon and tore open the wrapping paper. And in the box, he discovered something so magnificent, so marvelously fabulous:

A WIG.

He put it on and
raced to look in a mirror.

"*I'M* GORGEOUS!"

he declared.

After Noah's mom and dad showed him how to put the wig on properly, he braided it and twisted it and piled it on top of his head.

And then he and his dad and everyone else had a dance party where they tossed their hair back and forth.

He was *not* able to hang from a tree with it.

Still, it was the best birthday ever.

Exactly one year later,
Noah hopped into
the car to go get his
birthday haircut.

As he climbed into the barber's chair, the barber asked, "What'll it be?"

Noah replied,

"Just a little off the ends, please!"

CONVERSATION STARTERS

The Good Hair Day touches on themes of gender, identity, and self-expression.
We encourage you to explore these topics with your child to promote
inclusivity, acceptance, and respect for others.

Hair can look and be styled in many different ways. How do people you know wear their hair?
How do you like to wear your hair? Are there other styles you might like to try someday?

Can anyone choose to cut their hair short or grow their hair long? Why or why not?

What are some other ways that people can express themselves through their style?
(Hint: clothing, jewelry, accessories.)

What are some ways that you are different from other kids your age? What are some ways
you are the same?

How might you feel if you weren't allowed to play your favorite sport, participate in your
favorite activity, or paint with your favorite color because of your gender?

What are some ways that you can get to know and include a new friend who may seem very
different from you at first?

*Tips and conversation starters written by Dr. Danielle Vrieze, child psychologist
and assistant professor at the University of Minnesota Medical School*